THREE HALVES

A GAME OF THREE HALVES

A Collection of Balls-ups from The Beautiful Game

Charlie Croker

First published 2002 by Boxtree
an imprint of Pan Macmillan Ltd
Pan Macmillan, 20 New Wharf Road, London N1 9RR
Basingstoke and Oxford
Associated companies throughout the world
www.panmacmillan.com

ISBN 0 7522 6495 8

9 8 7 6 5 4 3 2 1

A CIP catalogue record for this book is available from
the British Library.

Design by seagulls
Printed and bound in Great Britain by Cox and Wyman Ltd,
Reading, Berkshire

Introduction

Some people discover at an early age that they're very, very good at kicking a football. This means they then give up on other activities that young people traditionally indulge in, such as getting an education. And so footballers grow up to say and do some silly things. And when they've finished playing, they become managers or commentators, for our continued amusement.

PLAYERS

Asked in Chelsea's programme questionnaire when was the last time he took public transport, George Weah replied: 'Two weeks ago I took a taxi.'

And asked in the Leeds United programme questionnaire which film star he would like to be washed up on a desert island with, Darren Huckerby replied: 'Robert De Niro.'

And asked in the Reading programme questionnaire who he would most like to meet, Graeme Murty replied: 'Joan of Arc – the one who rode naked through the streets.'

Ian Rush, noticing that a long-serving journalist was absent from a press conference, asked where he was.

'Unfortunately,' came the reply, 'he has very suddenly and unexpectedly passed on.'

'How did he die?' asked the Liverpool legend.

'It was the big "C".'

'Couldn't he swim?' asked Rush.

'A contract on a piece of paper,
saying you want to leave, is like
a piece of paper saying you want
to leave.'

– John Hollins

Journalist: 'What did you do after the Romanian defeat?'

David Seaman: 'We talked over everything, the things that went right and the things that didn't work out. Then we studied the videos very carefully.'

Journalist: 'Why do you think you lost, then?'

Seaman: 'Well, it were just one of those things.'

Filling in a credit card application form, Jason McAteer came to the question that asked: 'What is your position in the company?'

He put: 'Right back.'

'Germany are a very difficult
team to play – they had eleven
internationals out there today.'
– Steve Lomas

In 1999, Romanian midfielder Mario Bugeanu arrived home with his girlfriend. The couple were feeling particularly amorous, and couldn't wait to get inside the house before starting to make love. They couldn't even wait to get out of the garage. Or the car. Or indeed to turn off the engine.

The next morning the couple were found dead in the car by Mario's father. 'They appeared to be unaware of the dangers of carbon monoxide,' said police colonel Dumitru Secrieru.

Steve Howey, whose hair had started to turn grey, tried to dye it black. But failing to read the instructions on the bottle properly cost him dear: his hair tuRned purple and took three months to turn back to its old colour.

Lyon's David Linares put
eucalyptus oil on the coals at
a sauna, setting fire to the
building. He had to be treated
in hospital for second-degree
burns to his back and arms.

PLAYERS

'If there wasn't such a thing as
football we'd all be frustrated
footballers.'
                    – Mick Lyons

'I was disappointed to
leave Spurs, but quite
pleased that I did.'
                    – Steve Perryman

'Because of the booking,
I will miss the Holland game –
if selected.'
                    – Paul Gascoigne

'It's a shame half-time
came as early as it did.'
                    – Gordon Drury

'We've got to start winning
games now, instead of leaving it
until the games have run out.'
                    – Marc Edworthy

'I'd love to play for one
of those Italian teams
like Barcelona'
                    – Mark Draper.

Draper's sense of geography eventually sorted itself out, and he found himself playing in Spain, for Rayo Vallecano. His sense of language, however, still contrived to let him down. He urged his colleagues to 'permiso, permiso'. But he had looked up the wrong version of the word 'pass', and was in fact running around shouting 'driving licence, driving licence'.

On his first day at
Manchester United, Fabien
Barthez took a wrong turn
and ended up in Liverpool.

'I spent four indifferent
years at Goodison, but they
were great years.'
                    – Martin Hodge

'I would not be bothered if
we lost every game as long
as we won the league.'
                    - Mark Viduka

'He's put on weight and
I've lost it, and vice versa.'
                    - Ronnie Whelan

'If you don't believe you can win, there is no point in getting out of bed at the end of the day.'
— Neville Southall

'We lost because we didn't win.'
— Ronaldo

'I've had fourteen bookings this season – eight of which were my fault, but seven of which were disputable.'
– Paul Gascoigne

'You've got to believe that
you're going to win, and
I believe we'll win the World
Cup until the final whistle
blows and we're knocked out.'
                    – Peter Shilton

'I faxed a transfer request to
the club at the beginning of the
week, but let me state that I
don't want to leave Leicester.'
                    – Stan Collymore

PLAYERS

'I was watching the Blackburn game on TV on Sunday when it flashed on the screen that George [Ndah] had scored in the first minute at Birmingham. My first reaction was to ring him up. Then I remembered he was out there playing.'
– Ade Akinbiyi

PLAYERS

'It was a big relief off
my shoulder.'
                    - Paul Gascoigne

'I'm as happy as I can be -
but I have been happier.'
                    - Ugo Ehiogu

'All that remains is for a few
dots and commas to be crossed.'
                    - Mitchell Thomas

'Winning doesn't really
matter – as long as you win.'
                    – Vinnie Jones

'His return gives England
another key to its bow.'
                    – Stuart Pearce

'I took a whack on my left
ankle, but something told
me it was my right.'
                    – Lee Hendrie

⚽ **PLAYERS**

29

'If you're 0–0 down, there's no
one better to get you back on
terms than Ian Wright.'
                    – Robbie Earle

'Who should be there at
the far post but yours
truly, Alan Shearer.'
                    – Colin Hendry

'The opening ceremony was
good, although I missed it.'
                    – Graeme Le Saux

'One accusation you can't
throw at me is that I've
always done my best.'
                        – Alan Shearer

In 1914, Moses Russell moved into a new house after signing for Plymouth Argyle. His friend Jack Fowler offered to help him decorate it. Only when they'd worked all day and finished every room did Russell realize that they were in the wrong house.

Playing in a game during World War Two, Charlton goalkeeper Sam Bartram was tapped on the shoulder by a policeman, who proceeded to inform him that the game had been abandoned due to fog, and he was the only player left on the field.

'If you stand still there's
only one way to go, and
that's backwards.'
                    – Peter Shilton

When Uruguay's Hohberg
equalized for them in the
1954 World Cup semi-final
against Hungary, his teammates
congratulated him so vigorously
that they knocked him
unconscious.

PLAYERS' RELATIVES

The teenage Roy Sutcliffe
went for a trial at Manchester
United in 1950. He dreamed
of playing for the club, but as
the days and then weeks went
by and he heard nothing, it
dawned on him that his dream
was not to be. He got over
his disappointment, and
got on with his life.

In 1994, his mother Mabel, clearing out a drawer, found a letter that she'd forgotten to give to him when it was delivered in 1950. The now sixty-three-year-old Roy opened the envelope, to find that the letter was from Jimmy Murphy, Sir Matt Busby's talent scout, asking him to go back for another trial.

Alberto Cuero of Ecuador
was widely praised for his skill
in the 1999 South American
Under-17 Championships –
until his father announced
that he was really twenty.

MANAGERS

'Shearer could be at 100
per cent fitness, but not
peak fitness.'

                        – Graham Taylor

'I'm not going to make it
a target, but it's something
to aim for.'

        – Steve Coppell

'If we played like this
every week, we wouldn't
be so inconsistent.'

        – Bobby Robson

'Without picking out anyone
in particular, I thought Mark
Wright was tremendous.'

        – Graeme Souness

At his first match in charge of Nottingham Forest, Ron Atkinson emerged from the tunnel to a rapturous welcome from the home fans. Beaming, he soaked up the applause, posed for the crowd of press photographers . . . then went and sat in the away team's dugout.

'I'm not a believer in luck –
but I do believe you need it.'
                    – Alan Ball

'I am a firm believer that if you
score one goal, the other team
have to score two to win.'
                    – Howard Wilkinson

'The spirit he has shown has been second to none.'
  - Terry Venables on Terry Fenwick's drink-driving charge

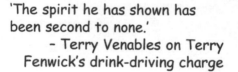

'There are two ways of getting the ball. One is from your own teammates, and that's the only way.'
                    – Terry Venables

'I would have to be deaf not to read the allegations.'
                    – Bobby Downes

'They had a dozen corners, maybe twelve – I'm guessing.'
– Craig Brown

'Our first goal was pure textile.'
– John Lambie

'We probably got on better with the likes of Holland, Belgium, Norway and Sweden, some of whom are not even European.'
– Jack Charlton

MANAGERS

'Playing with wingers is more
effective against European
sides like Brazil than English
sides like Wales.'
                    – Ron Greenwood

'When you are 4–0 up you
should never lose 7–1.'
                    – Lawrie McMenemy

'We are not putting our cape over the tunnel: we are putting our cape *in* the tunnel.'
                    – Howard Wilkinson

'What he's got is legs, which the other midfielders don't have.'
                    – Lennie Lawrence

'I promise results, not promises.'
— John Bond

'We must have had 99
per cent of the game.
It was the other 3 per cent
that cost us the match.'
— Ruud Gullit

'He's putting more distance between the goal-line and the penalty spot.'

– Ron Atkinson

'We didn't underestimate
them – they were a lot better
than we thought.'
                        – Bobby Robson

'When a player gets to
thirty, so does his body.'
                    – Glenn Hoddle

'OK, so we lost, but good
things can come from it –
negative and positive.'
                    – Glenn Hoddle

'Michael Owen is a goalscorer –
not a natural-born one, not
yet, that takes time.'
                    – Glenn Hoddle

'You weigh up the pros and cons
and try to put them into
chronological order.'
                    – Dave Bassett

'Today's top players only
want to play in London or for
Manchester United. That's
what happened when I tried to
sign Alan Shearer and he went
to Blackburn.'

– Graeme Souness

MANAGERS

'It would be foolish to believe
that automatic promotion is
automatic in any way
whatsoever.'
– Dave Bassett

'In one word, it is bloody
stupidity.'
– Claude Le Roy

'He's captain of Rangers,
and that's one of the
reasons he's captain.'
– Walter Smith

'Very few of us have any
idea whatsoever of what life
is like living in a goldfish bowl –
except, of course, for those
of us who are goldfish.'
                    – Graham Taylor

'The sight of opposing fans walking together down Wembley Way – you won't get that anywhere other than Wembley.'
— John Sillett

'David [Johnson] has scored 62 goals in 148 games for Ipswich and those statistics tell me that he plays games and scores goals.'
— David Platt

'I don't know what it's like
out there, but it's like an
ice rink out there.'
                    – Andy Kilner

'And I honestly believe
that we can go all the way
to Wembley . . . unless
somebody knocks us out.'
                    – Dave Bassett

MANAGERS

'We've got to the bottom
of Jonny Rowan's back,
it's his pelvis.'
                              – Lennie Lawrence

'Winning isn't the end
of the world.'
                              – David Pleat

'Certain people are for me,
certain people are pro me.'
                    – Terry Venables

'Hoddle hasn't been the Hoddle
we know. Neither has Robson.'
                    – Ron Greenwood

'What I said to them
at half time would be
unprintable on the radio.'
                    - Gerry Francis

COMMENTATORS

'The goals made such a difference to the way this game went.'

– John Motson

'Apart from their goals,
Norway haven't scored.'
— Terry Venables

'Batistuta gets most of
his goals with the ball.'
— Ian St John

'Ian Baird is dashing around like
a steam roller up front.'
                    – Martin Tyler

'Many clubs have a question
mark in the shape of an axe-
head hanging over them.'
                    – Malcolm McDonald

COMMENTATORS

'And with four minutes gone,
the score is already 0–0.'
                          – Ian Dark

'It's a tale of two systems,
John, and both exactly
the same.'
                          – Mark Lawrenson

'Never go for a 50–50 ball
unless you're 80–20 sure
of winning it.'

— Ian Darke

'Nicky Butt, he's another aptly
named player. He joins things,
brings one sentence to an end
and starts another.'

— Barry Davies

COMMENTATORS

'He's passing the ball
like Idi Amin.'

— Alan Parry

'He went through a
non-existent gap.'

— Clive Tyldesley

'Peru score their third,
and it's 3–1 to Scotland.'
                    – David Coleman

'And Rush, quick as a needle . . .
' – Ron Jones

'Poor Graham Shaw. It was
there for the asking and he
didn't give the answer.'
– Peter Jones

'Newcastle, of course, unbeaten
in their last five wins.'
                    – Brian Moore

'And he's got the icepack on
his groin there, so possibly not
the old shoulder injury.'
                    – Ray French

'I'm not saying he [David Ginola] is the best left winger in the Premiership, but there are none better.'
— Ron Atkinson

'An inch or two either side of the post and that would have been a goal.'
— Dave Basset, SKY Sports

'And then there was Johan
Cruyff, who at thirty-five has
added a whole new meaning to
the word Anno Domini.'
                    – Archie Macpherson

'Sporting Lisbon in their
green and white hoops, looking
like a team of zebras . . .'
                    – Peter Jones

COMMENTATORS

'. . . evoking memories,
particularly of days gone by.'
                        – Mike Ingham

'Bristol Rovers were 4–0
up at half time, with four
goals in the first half.'
                        – Tony Adamson

'Leeds are enjoying more possession now that they have the ball.'

— Simon Brotherton

'And Arsenal now have plenty of time to dictate the last few seconds.'

– Peter Jones

Ian St John: 'It's a real battle tomorrow with Brazil against Spain. What do you reckon, Bruce?'

Bruce Grobbelaar: 'Well, I've got to go for the Italians on this one, Saint.'

COMMENTATORS

'Mirandinha will have more shots this afternoon than both sides put together.'
– Malcolm McDonald

'That's football, Mike, Northern Ireland have had several chances and haven't scored but England have had no chances and scored twice.'
– Trevor Brooking

COMMENTATORS

'Merseyside derbies usually last ninety minutes and I'm sure today's won't be any different.'
— Trevor Brooking

'The symbol of peace . . . the pigeon!'
— RTE's Jimmy Magee at the 1982 World Cup finals opening ceremony.

COMMENTATORS

'He came on a free transfer
and has been giving good
value for money.'

– Clive Allen

'Whether that was a
penalty or not, the referee
thought otherwise.'

– Brian Moore

'Tottenham are trying
tonight to become the first
London team to win this cup.
The last team to do so was
the 1973 Spurs team.'

– Mike Ingham

'If history is going to repeat itself I should think we can expect the same again.'
                                        – Terry Venables

'Forest have now lost six matches without winning.'
                                        – David Coleman

'2-0 is a cricket score in Italy.'
                    – Alan Parry

'Ian Rush is deadly ten
times out of ten, but that
wasn't one of them.'
                    – Peter Jones

COMMENTATORS

'Vialli's absolutely certain that
he knows one way or the other
whether he'll score or not.'
                    – Jonathan Pearce

'Hagi has got a left foot
like Brian Lara's bat.'
                    – Don Howe

'We're not used to weather
in June in this country.'
— Jimmy Hill

'I think that France, Germany,
Spain, Holland and England will
join Brazil in the semi-finals.'
— Pelé

COMMENTATORS

Pelé was asked to name his favourite current Manchester United player, and replied: 'Michael Owen.'

'I'd be surprised if all twenty-two players are on the field at the end of the game – one's already been sent off.'
                    – George Best

'They'll perhaps finish in
the top three. I can't see
them finishing any higher.'

– Don Howe

'He's like all great players –
he's not a great player yet.'
                    – Trevor Francis

'There are no opportune times
for a penalty, and this is not
one of those times.'
                    – Jack Youngblood

COMMENTATORS

'Such a positive move by
Uruguay – bringing two players
off and putting two players on.'
                    – John Helm

'Referee Norlinger is
outstanding in the sense
that he stands out.'
                    – George Hamilton

'That youngster is playing well
beyond his nineteen years –
that's because he's twenty-one.'
                    – David Begg

'With eight minutes left, the
game could be won in the next
five or ten minutes.'
                    – Jimmy Armfield

'It wouldn't be a surprise to see Marseilles play a rough game, but it would be surprising if they did.'
— Chris Waddle

'It's the end of season curtain raiser.'
— Peter Withe

'They're still in the game, and they're trying to get back into it.'
— Jimmy Hill

⚽ COMMENTATORS

'There's Bergkamp standing
on the halfway line, with his
hands on his hips, flailing
his arms about.'

– John Scales

'That's twice now he [Terry
Phelan] has got between
himself and the goal.'

– Brian Marwood

'They didn't change positions, they just moved the players around.'
— Terry Venables

'If you're going to score one goal or less, you're not going to get your victories.'
— Trevor Brooking

'It's one of the greatest goals ever, but I'm surprised that people are talking about it being the goal of the season.'
— Andy Gray

'If Glenn Hoddle said one word
to his team at half time, it was
concentration and focus.'
                    – Ron Atkinson

'Germany are probably,
arguably, undisputed
champions of Europe.'
                    – Bryan Hamilton

COMMENTATORS

'We are about as far away from the penalty box as the penalty box is from us.'
                                                    – Tom Tyrell

'Owen runs like a rabbit chasing after . . . what do rabbits run after? They run after nothing . . . well, running after other rabbits.'
                                                    – Tom Tyrell

'That tie is a potential potato skin.'
                                                    – Alan Hansen

BARRY DAVIES

'Cantona's expression is speaking the whole French dictionary without saying a word.'

'Lukic saved with his foot, which is all part of the goalkeeper's arm.'

BARRY DAVIES

'Poland nil, England nil, though England are now looking the better value for their nil.'

'The crowd think that Todd handled the ball . . . they must have seen something that nobody else did.'

'If it had gone in, it would have been a goal.'

'The Dutch fans look like a huge jar of marmalade.'

'That's lifted the crowd up into the air.'

'Jim Leighton is looking as sharp as a tank.'

'Izzet . . . no is the answer.'

INTERVIEWERS

Arsene Wenger was asked if he thought Arsenal would have to finish above Manchester United to win the Premiership. 'You have to finish above everyone to win the Premiership,' he pointed out.

Elton Welsby: '*Magnifique*, Eric.'

Eric Cantona: 'Oh, do you speak French?'

Elton Welsby: '*Non.*'

Jim Rosenthal: 'So what's an American doing playing in goal for Millwall?'

American goalie: 'I'm trying to keep the ball out.'

INTERVIEWERS

JOURNALISTS

'The England captaincy fell
to [Beckham] not by default,
but through an obvious
lack of alternatives.'
                    – David Walsh

The *Peterborough Evening Telegraph* had to abandon their Spot the Ball competition in February 1995. They had left the ball in the photograph.

BOOKMAKERS

The Ontario Lottery Corporation took bets on four English matches in 1995, and lost £365,000. They had believed them to be evening kick-offs. But they were actually afternoon matches, and the punters had placed their bets already knowing the results.

CRIMINALS

Thieves raided the changing rooms while a game was being played at Brampton FC's ground near Huntingdon in November 1999 – and were caught by twenty-three policemen.
The game was between Cambridgeshire Police and the Metropolitan Police's NW Division.

CRIMINALS

The Thai criminals who kidnapped businessman Chi Chong Yi accidentally let him escape when they fell asleep after watching the 1998 World Cup Final.

ROYALS

In February 2000, Prince Philip met Leroy Thornhill of The Prodigy, who was wearing an Arsenal shirt with the name of the team's sponsor emblazoned across the front. Prince Philip asked Thornhill about his club 'Dreamcast'.

ROYALS

FIREMEN

A fireman called to put out
a fire at Birmingham City's
ground in January 1942 poured
kerosene instead of water
onto it, and burned down the
whole stand.

AGENTS

When John Hartson's recent
move to Spurs broke down
because of a knee problem, his
agent moaned: 'Their medical
examination was so stringent
only Mother Teresa
would have passed it.'

DIRECTORS

Legendary Liverpool player Billy Liddell was famous for being a strict teetotaller. He refused even to sip champagne from the cup when Liverpool won the 1947 league championship. When he broke the record of 429 league games for the club, the directors presented him with a cocktail cabinet filled with every kind of alcoholic drink.

Following problems that had received widespread publicity within the game, Brighton were forced to play their home games at Gillingham's ground. One of Cardiff City's directors went to see his team play Brighton - and actually went to Brighton. He then made his way to Gillingham, where he proudly surveyed the fans in their blue and white colours, and commented: 'We've got some good travelling support tonight.' Someone had to point out to him that they were the Brighton fans.

DIRECTORS

CHAIRMEN

Elton John sent Watford season-ticket holders a letter describing the team's first season in the Premiership as a 'never-to-be repeated experience'.

Arsenal chairman Peter Hill-Wood at the shareholders' annual general meeting: 'Everyone and his uncle knows who is coming, but we have made an undertaking not to name our new coach.'

Someone from the floor: 'Who have you made that undertaking to?'

PH-W: 'Arsene Wenger and his club.'

CHAIRMEN

FANS

Among the items with which Luis Figo was pelted by irate Barcelona fans when he returned there with arch-rivals Real Madrid were two mobile telephones.

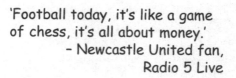

'Football today, it's like a game of chess, it's all about money.'
– Newcastle United fan,
Radio 5 Live

In May 1993, a Newcastle United fan living in America was very excited about his team's forthcoming evening match against Oxford – it could clinch them promotion to the top division. He resigned from his job, spent his savings on a flight back to England, got a taxi from Heathrow to Oxford, and arrived at Oxford just in time for the kick-off. The game was actually being played at Newcastle.

Ian 'Fergie' Russell, one of Hamilton Academical's best-known fans, was trying to hitch a lift home from a game at Brechin. The team coach passed, and stopped to offer him a lift. Fergie gratefully climbed on board. But he then couldn't stop himself from berating the players for that afternoon's defeat, with the result that the coach stopped again ten minutes later, and he was thrown off.

FANS' RELATIVES

A Newcastle fan noticed that the two seats next to him had been empty for every match that season. Puzzled why anyone would spend all that money on two season tickets and never use them, his confusion deepened when at the Boxing Day home match a middle-aged man and his teenage son occupied the seats.

Unable to contain his curiosity any longer, at half-time he turned to the man and asked why he hadn't used the season tickets until now. 'They were a Christmas present from the wife,' replied the man with a weary expression, 'and she didn't actually tell us about them until Christmas Day.'

FANS' RELATIVES

FANS' FRIENDS

Watching his team at Anfield, Watford fan Patrick Nugent was alarmed to hear a tannoy call saying that there had been a telephone call for him, and would he report to reception as soon as possible. He made his way anxiously there, only to be told that his neighbour had rung to say he was going away, and would Patrick mind looking after his cat?

An irritated Nugent then returned to his seat to discover that he had missed Watford scoring the only goal of the match.

KEVIN KEEGANS

'I don't think there is anybody bigger or smaller than Maradona.'

'They compare Steve McManaman to Steve Highway and he's nothing like him, but I can see why – it's because he's a bit different.'

'Sometimes there are too many generals and not enough, er, people waving to the generals as they, er, walk past.'

'That would have been a goal
if it wasn't saved.'

'There's only one team going
to win it now, and that's
England.' In a 1998 World Cup
match, two minutes before
Dan Petrescu scored
Romania's winner.

KEVIN KEEGANS

'The ref was vertically fifteen yards away.'

'In some ways, cramp is worse than having a broken leg.'

'The thirty-three- or thirty-four-year-olds will be thirty-six or thirty-seven by the time the next World Cup comes around, if they're not careful.'

KEVIN KEEGANS

'Argentina won't be at Euro 2000 because they're from South America.'

'Despite his white boots, he has real pace . . .'

Born on the 30th of July 1966 to an English mother and a West German father, Charlie Croker has always had an understandably love-hate relationship with the game of football. After developing a childhood reputation as one of the best in his position (goalpost), he went on to win Dunstable Scout Group's Ball Boy of the Year award three seasons in a row. A dark episode was his expulsion from Nottingham Forest's cheerleading troupe (for looking too feminine), but in recent years Croker has made a triumphant return to the footballing scene as Chief Grooming Attendant to Des Lynam's moustache.

He lives in Slough with his cat and two thousand pictures of Alan Shearer.